FAVOR FOR HIS WIFE
BY
STACY-DEANNE
VENUS RAY

GW00585103

Readers: Thanks so much for choosing my book! I would be very appreciative if you would leave reviews when you are done. Much love!

Email: stacydeanne1@aol.com

Website: Stacy's Website [1]

---

1. https://www.stacy-deanne.com/

Facebook: Stacy's Facebook Profile[2]
Twitter: Stacy's Twitter[3]

To receive book announcements subscribe to Stacy's mailing

list: Mailing List[4]

---

2.   https://www.facebook.com/stacy.deanne.5

3.   https://twitter.com/stacydeanne

4.   https://stacybooks.eo.page/cjjy6

NOTE TO READERS:

Thanks for picking up this book. The Sex in the Wild West Series is a historical interracial erotic short story series featuring black women and white men couples. Each book stands alone. This means that you don't have to read them in any specific order! If you enjoy this story then make sure to check the webpage dedicated to the series: CLICK HERE[5]

On this page you will see the books released as well as books that are upcoming so you can preorder. You can also keep up with the series on its Amazon series page under Stacy-Deanne or Venus Ray.

IMPORTANT: You can also sign up for the *Sex in the Wild West Series* mailing list. You will get an email whenever a new book releases! Note, if you are a subscriber to Stacy's regular mailing list then you still need to sign up for this one if you want information on this series. Stacy will not be sending mailings about this series to her existing list since these books are erotica.

Sign up here: https://stacybooks.eo.page/rd687

Enjoy!

CHAPTER ONE

Wilkerson, Montana 1895

Delia jumped from her seat at the Moonlight House, her gaze glued to the petite white woman wearing a raggedy shawl around her thin shoulders. Her pale skin probably could shine like porcelain if not for it wearing the dust of wherever she came from. You could still tell she'd be desirable if she fixed herself up and threw on a bit of makeup. Not too much because looking natural was the key, but just something to bring more attention to the lady's delicate features and light-brown eyes.

But with the way the frantic woman stood at the batwing doors, with her eyes wide as if someone had just pulled a Winchester rifle on her, something told Delia the last thing on this woman's mind was makeup.

Delia sashayed through the thick smell of tobacco and cannabis, while painted Negro women draped themselves over the rowdy cowboys playing poker.

The Moonlight House was the only colored brothel on this side of Montana and the only
place where a black woman could make a decent wage besides being a maid and no, Delia wasn't no one's maid. Never had been and never would be. She'd spent her life seeing the women in her family start off as young as 12 cleaning up after white folks and she wore that would never be her.

Yeah, she might fuck the hell out of a white man. Might go down on him and even add a little rimming if he looked clean enough. But cleaning after someone like some modern-day slave? Hell no. Especially when so many men said Delia had the best pussy in town. Better than any white or Negro woman and she'd made this brothel a lot of money, though she only had a small percentage to show for it.

The white lady gawked at Delia, looking her up and down as if she'd seen a ghost. Maybe she'd never seen a painted Negro woman before, or could she have come by for her *own* pleasure?

Delia put on her most enticing smile, just in case. Dick or pussy. She didn't care as long as she got paid.

"Can I help you, sweetheart?" Delia asked the shivering woman. "Looks like you're lost."

Strands of the woman's dirty-blonde hair had gotten loose from her bun. "Why would you
say I'm lost?"

Delia looked her over. "Because we don't get many white ladies down here in
case you didn't notice." She raised her voice over the hollering, hooting and clay poker chips being slammed on the tables.

3

"You... you're beautiful," the woman said. "The prettiest one in here."

Delia chuckled. "Maybe that's why I make the most money. What do you need, honey? Because this ain't the place for an innocent little thing like you."

The woman rubbed her dirty hands together. Obviously, she came from a ranch or farm. "I need a woman. I went to the white brothel first, but they turned me away. No woman would even discuss it further once I worked up the courage to ask the favor."

"Favor?" Delia's ears perked up because this woman sounded desperate and desperate people always gave the biggest rewards. "Well, I'd be interested in hearing this offer. I make no promises, though. Follow me." She led the lady upstairs and through the hallway. Moans, groans and shrieking had become the theme song of the place.

"My Lord." The lady covered her ears. "Is it like this all the time?"

Delia opened the door to her room. "It's slow tonight if you can believe it. Come in." She twisted into the plain wooden room with just a bed by the window and a table for her to freshen up. "It ain't fancy, but it's mine. I'm proud to have my own. I work hard to keep a place here."

"I imagine." The lady grimaced as she stared at the bare space. "You live here?"

"Yes, I do." Delia sat at the table and crossed her legs, her corset choking the life out of her. "Some girls don't, though. They just come here to, you know... do their business."

"I couldn't ever do *this*." The woman shook her head. "I wouldn't have the nerve."

"Sure you could. Whoring ain't no different from any other job. Besides, you don't know what you can do until you have to do it. Sit down. Share with me the reason you came."

The lady looked at Delia's bed as if she thought it was diseased, then timidly sat on it. "My name is Mary-Jane Lipnicki. My husband is Tom Lipnicki. We have no kids."

Delia nodded, filling her smoking pipe with tobacco.

"We got married ten years ago." Mary-Jane cleared her throat. "I was twenty, and he was

thirty."

Delia sucked the pipe, studying Mary-Jane.

"He's a traveling salesman. Makes a decent living... when he's working."

"Salesman?" Delia puffed smoke. "I thought you lived on a ranch or something with as dirty as you are."

Mary-Jane examined her hands. "I'm a homemaker and Tom travels all the time, but his work's been slow."

"This is fascinating. But what does this have to do with why you're here?"

Mary-Jane swallowed. "Will you have sex with my husband?"

Delia chuckled. "That's a new one. Usually it's the man who invites me into the master bed."

"I wouldn't be here if I didn't have a good excuse." Mary-Jane fidgeted. "I can't please my husband. It's been months since we laid down with one another."

A woman's pleasurable shrieks erupted from down the hall, breaking Delia's thoughts.

"My husband is a good man. A hard-working man, but I have no sex drive anymore. It's not his fault, so don't blame him. And he is a wonderful lover."

"No sex drive?" Delia sat back, holding the pipe. "I'd die. What's wrong with you?"

"I don't know."

"Sure you do. Never met a woman who didn't know *why* she couldn't have sex."

"This is about my husband, not me. We aren't rich, of course, but I'll pay you and you can even stay at the house for free as long as you want." Mary-Jane glanced around. "It's small, but nicer than this. I think you'll like it."

"You don't know me from Adam. I could get to your house, slice both of your throats and take *all* your money."

"You could. But I doubt you would. I guess it's your face and your nature that makes me trust you."

Delia groaned. "You don't even know my name."

"What *is* your name?"

"Delia." She laid the pipe in the tray of ashes. "Delia Frank."

"How old are you, Delia?"

"Twenty-four. And if you wanna ask me how long I've been a whore, since fifteen."

"Fifteen? I see."

"Don't do that."

"Do what?"

"Look at me like you pity me. I'm having the time of my life, lady."

"It's just fifteen is so young."

"Men like 'em young." Delia rocked her foot. "No one's paying money to spend time with

somebody's old mammy."

"What do you say?" Mary-Jane batted her eyes. "Will you take the offer?"

Delia thought it over. She was tiring of this place and if she liked the husband, a long-term deal could be very rewarding. Plus, she pitied Mary-Jane. Such a sad, pathetic little woman. You had to be to hire a whore for your own husband. She claimed she was doing this to help Tom but it was obvious Mary-Jane was the one who needed the most help in that marriage.

"Tell you what." Delia stood. "Stay here for the night, and take me to meet your husband in the morning. I need to see if we have chemistry then we'll go from there."

"You mean it?" Mary-Jane ran to Delia and hugged her, almost knocking the taller Delia over. "Oh, thank you! Tom's gonna love you. I know he will."

CHAPTER TWO

The following morning, Delia rode alongside Mary-Jane in the open carriage, wondering what the hell she'd gotten herself into. Mary-Jane steered them across the grassy plains and graveled roads, all the while yakking about her marriage. She admitted she didn't want to get married like most young women didn't. She'd married to be decent. It was the complete opposite of Delia's philosophy. She'd spent her life going against the supposed norms of society, unlike women who typically ran toward them.

Delia had to admit the ride was lovely. It had been a long time since she'd been in this area of the town. Instead of hearing moans, groans, and glasses breaking, she enjoyed the clippity-clop of the horse's shoes against the pavement, the birds singing, and the smell of nature.

And the quiet. A quiet she'd never experienced before.

"Don't be frightened or anything when we get there." Mary-Jane worked the reins. "Tom is a delightful man. He's handsome too. I'm sure you'll like him."

"I don't care about looks." Delia wobbled with the movement of the carriage. "As long as he treats me right, it's fine. I'm here to do a job."

"You're doing me a favor, actually." Mary-Jane's brown eyes filled up with sincerity. "And I'm more grateful than you could ever know."

They rode in silence for the new few moments before Delia broke it.

"Do you love your husband, Mary-Jane? It's not my business, but I'm curious."

"Course I do," she said in a shaky voice. "Tom's been very good to me. He works hard and provides me with a good life. Any wife would be lucky to have him."

"Yet, you don't seem to be. Usually when a woman doesn't let her husband touch her, it's for a reason."

Mary-Jane sat up straight, nostrils flaring. "It's not just me who won't let my husband get close."

Delia gaped. "Tom refuses *you* too?"

"Perhaps he finds it hard to forgive me for not being able to provide something he's always wanted." She swallowed tears. "The true reason he married me."

"Kids?" Delia whispered. "You're barren?"

Mary-Jane closed her eyes. "I hate that term."

"Whatever you call it, you can't have kids." Delia overlooked her. "Are you sure it's you?"

"Doctors confirmed that something just don't work right in my body. It'll be impossible for me to get pregnant. Then if I did, I'm most likely to lose the baby."

"Nonsense. You're a woman with the biology of one. No doctor can tell you, you can't have kids just because it ain't happened yet."

Mary-Jane looked at her, her loose strands blowing in her face.

"Are you religious?" Delia asked.

"Of course." Mary-Jane grimaced as if insulted by the mere question. "Born and raised a Christian and will die as one. That's why you're here. Because of my belief that you please your husband, no matter what. A happy husband is a happy wife. If he's unhappy, then so am I."

"Just because it ain't happened don't mean you won't have a baby." Delia shrugged. "But if you just give up you surely won't."

Mary-Jane snickered. "Are *you* a Christian?"

Delia straightened her shoulders. "I believe in God, yes. Now whether I practice the word is a whole different story."

The women laughed.

"Here we are. Up yonder." Mary-Jane blushed as she steered the horse through a crooked, dirt road toward the saddest little house Delia had ever seen. Just a pile of wood with no life and even less personality.

"Whoa." Mary-Jane stopped the carriage. "Well, what do you think? I know it ain't much to look at, but it's home, and we got all we need here."

Delia couldn't get over how drab everything looked. The grass was dry and brown, as if they hadn't tended to it in months. The roof on the house needed fixing, and the porch steps looked like they would fall apart any minute. Along with Mary-Jane's pitiful attire, it didn't add up.

Tom was supposedly a salesman, and they made good money. Either they squandered every penny he brought home or they just didn't give a shit about anything anymore. They'd given up on not only their marriage, but they'd stopped living.

Delia felt even worse for Mary-Jane. To where she didn't know if she could take her money in good faith because, frankly, they looked like they needed every dime.

"Delia, come here!" Mary-Jane ran out on the porch and Delia hadn't realized she'd even

went into the house. "I want you to meet my husband, Tom."

Getting her mind back on the job at hand, Delia climbed out of the carriage just as a man walked out.

Delia squinted, not believing who was in front of her eyes and by the way he looked, he was just as surprised. Mary-Jane had called him Tom, but to Delia he was "Mike" and she'd never forgotten him or never would. It had only been a few months since she saw him in Carter, Montana. Tall and thin, he'd seem to have the weight on his shoulders when they met. He'd been so full of hopelessness on that Friday, but by the end of their weekend together, he was like a kid in a candy store.

He said Delia rekindled his fire. Made him see life in a whole new world. He claimed he'd fallen in love with her in two days and wanted to take her to a better life.

Course Delia hadn't believed him at first because many men had told her that after spending time with her. Again, she had the best pussy around.

But as soon as Tom left and she could no longer feel his soft pale skin or look into his blazing blue eyes, she knew she'd made the biggest mistake of her life because she'd fallen in love with him as well. And she'd been too much of a coward to do anything about it.

Tom swallowed, looking at the unsuspecting Mary-Jane and then back at Delia. He looked at Delia like he did the day he left, face full of despair because Delia told him to go back to his wife because that's where he belonged.

She held in tears, cursing that she didn't take him up on his offer to leave with him when she had a chance. And now she'd met his wife, the one he couldn't connect with because of their issues. And damn it, Delia liked her. She pitied her and couldn't bear to tell her the truth after what Mary-Jane had just shared with her.

"Come on over, girl." Mary-Jane waved Delia over with a big smile.

Delia took delicate steps toward the house.

"Delia Frank?" Mary-Jane gestured to the handsome black-haired man beside her. "This is my husband, Tom Lipnicki."

Tom didn't wait until Delia made it up the steps. He raced down to greet her. He almost hugged her, but then seemed to remember his wife was right behind him and extended his hand instead.

"Delia?" He didn't say her name, but *breathed* it instead. "It is... so nice to meet you. Welcome to our home."

Delia took his hand and that one touch drained her from head to toe and had her more exhausted than an all-night fuck. His touch took her right back to that weekend and the naughty things they'd done in the name of passion. How was it possible, after all the men who'd touched her body, none had ever truly touched her like Mike had.

Or Tom. *Tom.*

She didn't know that one weekend in Carter, Montana, at the invitation of an old friend would lead to this.

"Tom." Delia's breath quivered as he caressed her hand with the top of his thumb. "It's nice to meet you. You don't look like a 'Tom.'" She let go of his hand, squinting. "You look more like a 'Mike.'"

He pulled back, pressing his thin lips together. Embarrassment gleaming from his clean-shaven face. "Mike is my middle name."

"Imagine that!" Mary-Jane ran down the porch, giggling. "How did you know that, Delia?"

She faked a chuckle. "Just seemed like 'Mike' fit him."

Tom stared at Delia as if Mary-Jane wasn't even there, and Delia dropped her gaze to throw off any suspicion.

"Did you get along all right, honey?" Mary-Jane asked Tom. "While I was gone?"

"You were only gone overnight." He kept his gaze on Delia. "I'm a big boy. I can take care of myself."

"Course you are, but you must be starving and so am I." Mary-Jane shook Delia's arm. "I'm sure you want some breakfast too, Delia. I'll get some food going. How about some biscuits and gravy and steak and eggs?"

Just hearing it made Delia's stomach growled.

"That's sounds great." Delia smiled at her. "But please don't go to any trouble on my account."

"Nonsense. You're doing me a great favor and I am so grateful." She hugged Delia. "Thank you."

Delia nodded. "You're welcome."

"I'll be right back." Mary-Jane ran up the porch. "Make yourself at home, Delia! The

outhouse is out back." Mary-Jane hurried inside and closed the door.

Suffocating from Tom's stare, Delia rushed away from him.

"Wait." He grabbed her. "Please."

"Let me go." She pushed him away. "Don't touch me again."

"That'll be impossible to do. You remember why you're here, don't you?"

She held her breath as she faced him. "Everything about you was a lie!"

"No... wait, okay—"

"Mike isn't your name. And you said you were some musician from Wyoming passing through Carter for a gig."

"I *am* a musician..." He grabbed his suspenders. "Just not by trade, but it's a passion."

"And you said you were from Wyoming, but obviously you weren't."

"Come on, Delia. Think. You've been with many Johns. You know how this works. How many give you their real names or proper occupations?"

"It's different." She sniffled. "I thought you were real and that what we shared was real, but it was a lie!"

"It's not a lie!" He grabbed her. "Delia, I love you. I care about Mary-Jane, but I've never, ever loved her. We married out of obligation and because it was the proper thing to do. Every thing I said to you that weekend was the truth. Every touch and every kiss, I meant it all. I've missed you so much and I tried to find you. I tried."

"You didn't try hard enough seeing how I'm right here in the same town. So Mary-Jane is the wife you were complaining about? The loveless marriage you're stuck in where you had me feeling so sorry for you?"

"Don't you see?" He pulled her in even closer. "We belong together, Delia. That's why you're here with me. God stepped in and made this all happen."

"No."

"*No?*" He chuckled. "You think this is a coincidence? My wife brought me an angel."

"No, she brought you a whore." She shook from his grasp. "That's all I am."

"Not to me. You've never been a whore to me. I love you, Delia." He locked his arms around her. "And I won't let you go again."

Mary-Jane walked out, interrupting the kiss. "Oh, I see you're getting acquainted already." She smiled, but it was obvious seeing Tom holding Delia made Mary-Jane uncomfortable. "Um, breakfast will be ready soon. Everything is on."

Delia flounced away from Tom. "That sounds nice and it smells heavenly. I apologize for any disrespect."

"No." Mary-Jane waved her dishrag. "Not at all. I want you two to get to know each other, so you'll be comfortable."

Tom stood behind Delia, pressing his erection against her.

"Uh, I'd like to see your lovely home." Delia rushed up the porch.

"Okay." Mary-Jane giggled. "But it ain't much to see."

CHAPTER THREE

"Mm." Delia bit into the tender steak. "Mary-Jane, you didn't have to go through so much trouble. This breakfast is probably the best meal I've had in ages."

"I'm so glad." She gushed. "We rarely have company, so I'm glad I could oblige."

Delia cleared her throat, trying to thwart Tom's gaze, but he hadn't turned away from her once. "I wish I could cook like this," Delia joked. "It's not one of my talents."

"And we know what your talents *are*." Tom raised an eyebrow, sucking scrambled eggs off his fork. "Don't we?"

Delia fidgeted, glancing at Mary-Jane, who obviously struggled to not seem offended.

"Excuse me." Mary-Jane wiped her mouth as she rose. "Duty calls. I'll be right back." She went outside.

"Stop it, Tom," Delia whispered. "You don't need to rub it in her face."

"I mean no malice, but I can't keep my eyes off you." He took her hand. "What's the problem? My wife brought you here for me. It's not like we're sneaking behind her back."

She yanked her hand away. "I don't think I can do this."

"What?" He grimaced. "You have to. Mary-Jane has paid you and besides, you want me as much as I want you."

She laid her fork on the plate. "It doesn't seem right."

"We are fate, Delia." He kissed her hand. "You know it, I know it, and Mary-Jane knows it too."

"But we're lying to her if we don't tell her the truth. She thinks we're strangers."

He let her hand go and went back to eating. "Why bring it up if it's not necessary? I can play the game if *you* can."

"Ah, I see. Is that what you were doing with me in Carter? Playing the game? You sure you're a traveling salesman and not a gambler?"

"I apologize for nothing. Not our weekend and not how I'm acting now. Delia, you possessed me. I haven't been the same since we met. I tried to come here and play the husband again, but that one smidge of happiness you and I shared showed me how miserable I really am."

"Mary-Jane's a good woman. She cares about you so much she'd bring me here to make you happy. What about *her*? You blame her for not being able to have kids?"

"Why shouldn't I?" He chewed. "When it's something any woman should be able to do. I bet
    you can have children."

She scoffed. "Oh, how can you be so cruel? Is this the man you really are?"

He exhaled. "I don't mean to be cruel, but I'm numb to it now, that's all. I live with this every day, Delia. You're on the outside looking in. You don't have the right to judge me."

Mary-Jane walked in. "Okay, I apologize." She sat.

"No, that's fine." Delia smiled.

"Tell us more about yourself, Delia," Mary-Jane said. "Um, do you like your profession?"

"Yes." She beamed with pride. "I enjoy what I do very much."

Tom smiled as he took a slow sip from his tin cup.

"It's not true what people think. About whores. That we're ashamed. We're not ashamed because we don't worry about what society thinks of us. See, people expect us to be worthless and less than. Especially when you're a Negro. Besides, it was either becoming a maid or a whore and I'm nobody's maid."

Mary-Jane and Tom chuckled.

"So, what do you do?"

"Mary-Jane," Tom scolded.

She laughed. "I meant, what things do you like to do *outside* of work, Delia?"

"I like to travel. I've made friendships with men from out of town and they take me places or invite me to come visit them."

"Really?" Mary-Jane propped her elbow on the table, staring at Delia as if she were the most fascinating thing she'd ever seen. "I've never been outside of Wilkerson myself. Tom and I made some plans to travel in the summer, but he had to work."

He cut into his steak. "If I don't work, then food isn't on the table."

"I wasn't criticizing you, dear." Mary-Jane patted his hand. "I was just saying it didn't work out."

Delia spoke to cut the tension, "Know what I like about my profession? That everyone is treated the same. To men, I'm just a whore. No one cares if you're a Negro or uneducated. All they want is what you can deliver between the sheets. You do that well, and you got a good career ahead of you."

Mary-Jane blushed. "Um, I imagine you've been with a lot of men?"

"More than I can count. Does that bother you?"

"No. You are, uh... safe?"

Delia grinned. "I am clean as a whistle, Mary-Jane. You don't have to worry about that."

"Do you have any hopes and dreams beyond your career choice?" Mary-Jane chewed. "Anything you'd like to do after you retire?"

"In my line of work you're old at thirty, so I don't have too many years left." Delia wiggled her fingers. "I'm definitely gonna travel and I might get married."

Tom looked up at her.

"Married?" Mary-Jane chewed slower. "Why would you wanna get married?"

"You think whores don't want marriage? Course we do. We want what most women want. Who doesn't crave a good man to love her like she's the only woman in the world?"

"You can definitely find that, Delia." Tom winked as he chewed. "If you look hard enough. Sometimes it's right in front of you."

Delia cut her gaze back to Mary-Jane. "I dream of a wonderful husband, a nice house and kids."

Mary-Jane's face dropped.

"Oh, God." Delia shook her head. "I'm so sorry, Mary-Jane. I didn't mean to—"

"No, it's fine." She wiggled in the chair. "Why should my plight take away your dreams? I wish you all the happiness in the world, Delia. And I think you'd make a great mother."

Delia smiled. "You do?"

Mary-Jane smiled. "I *do*."

****

After breakfast, Delia walked out on the porch to let her food go down and to enjoy the peace and quiet. She didn't even have time to sit down before Tom popped out and closed the door behind him.

"All that stuff you just told my wife. About you wanting marriage and kids? A man who will

love you like you're the only woman in the world?" He snatched her hand. "Well, that's me, Delia.

He's right here."

"Tom, please."

"No man will ever love you the way I do. I know you feel it too."

"Damn it." She closed her eyes. "Why can't I control my heart like so many other things in my life? Why did you even have to come along? I was doing fine without you!"

"We were both lost, and we needed to find each other to see that." He stood erect, letting her go. "That's why I've made my decision. I can't stay in this marriage another minute. My body is ripping in half because of how much I want you. That's the pain I'm in."

She turned and leaned over the porch railing. "What are you proposing to do about it?"

"I wanna give you your dream." He pressed against her back. "Be the husband you want and

deserve. But I can't do that with Mary-Jane in the way."

Delia turned around, pushing her curls out of her face though the breeze was determined to

keep them there. "What are you saying?"

"I'm leaving Mary-Jane. I'm gonna go right in there and tell her the truth."

"No, Tom." She grabbed his arm. "You can't do that. She'll be devastated—"

"I can't live like this anymore, Delia." He grabbed his head. "I'm going insane! I'm sorry that Mary-Jane can't have kids, but I can't forgo my happiness and be with her just to make her feel better."

"And you call yourself a Christian? Bad enough you cheated on her, but you want to leave her too? I thought when you got married, it was forever."

"God doesn't want us lying to ourselves either, and that's what I've been doing, pretending I can make this work. No. I can't stay with her any longer. Think of *her*, Delia. She deserves better."

"But I *don't*?"

"What?"

"If Mary-Jane deserves better than you, why don't I?"

"I *meant* she deserves a man who loves her as much as I love you." He rubbed his thumb against her lips. "We can't fight this anymore, Delia. I love you so much. Everything I say is true."

CHAPTER FOUR

Tom stroked Delia's hair and did something a man hadn't done since she'd last seen Tom. He kissed her. So gently and so lovingly to where she felt like she'd floated to another planet.

Men never kissed her because, kissing was more intimate than fucking and even though they could plunge their dicks inside of her, they couldn't stand the thought of putting their mouths to hers.

For all that big talk during breakfast about how much Delia loved her profession, of course there were aspects of it she couldn't stand as well. She hated being treated like an object. Like a cup for a man to piss in and then throw away. Sometimes she wanted to be held after sex and not pushed aside as if she had a disease. She was so sick of being judged by the same men who thought she was good enough to fuck, but not worthy enough to talk to.

Tom had been different. She knew that the first time she met him when he walked into the colored section of the tavern in Carter and sat right by her. Everyone else knew she was a whore and treated her as such. But Tom never did. He treated her like a person and he didn't care about her faults, only the way she made him feel. And within his kisses, she felt everything he said about loving her was true. You can lie, but you can't fake the emotion behind a kiss.

He pushed her against the house and stroked her body over her clothes. He panted, as if it excited him beyond belief just to hold her.

This was what she'd been missing. It had been a long time since she'd been a virgin, but Tom made her feel like one. Since they last saw each other, her feelings for him had gotten stronger whether or not she wanted to admit it and she couldn't fight them anymore.

She grabbed his face, smashing her lips against his. They stood so close that she felt his heartbeat and hers pounded so hard she thought it would bust out of her chest. "I love you, Tom."

Her saying the words opened the door to a new world. She'd no longer deny herself the very happiness anyone in the world deserved. She was a whore, but she was a good person. A person with dreams and hopes, like everyone else.

"I've missed your body so much." Sweating, Tom unwrapped her shawl, revealing the raunchy dress that hugged her figure. "Mm." He kissed down her neck and then across her plump brown cleavage, whispering sweet nothings.

Delia closed her eyes, losing herself on the wave of passion. Remembering what it was like to

be wanted for more than her body, but also her soul.

"Ride me." Tom pulled her down on the dusty planks, the wood squeaking underneath them. "Like you did in Carter. Don't stop until you've drained me dry."

He didn't have to give her instructions. She'd been dreaming of that dick since they parted. Tom completely undressed and she stared at his pale, tall body. To some women, he might've been too thin, but Delia found him perfect and she couldn't get enough of just looking at him.

She leaned over him and took his long, meaty member into her mouth.

"Oh, yes." He pushed his hand into her curls.

Sucking his dick took Delia right back to their magical weekend.

He moaned. "I've missed your mouth so much."

Delia licked and smacked, staring in his eyes as she pleasured him. She loved looking at a man's eyes while sucking him. It was the only way to see his true gratification.

"If I could marry you right now, I would," Tom said. "What an unfair world we live in to not be able to marry because of our color."

She massaged his cock. "I'd marry you in a heartbeat. You're the master of my soul. Of course I love you, Tom. I'll never love another."

He raised his black eyebrow. "Then show me how much you've missed me, my love. Right here."

She looked toward the shut door. Mary-Jane could come out any minute and even though she'd brought Delia there for this purpose, Delia felt guilty.

"It's okay." Tom caressed her cheek. "She wants us to do this, remember? She wants me to be happy."

He was right. This was all Mary-Jane's idea and here was Delia thinking more about her feelings than her own. If Mary-Jane couldn't handle this, she shouldn't have opened the door. Delia would not deprive herself of being with the only man she ever loved.

She lifted her skirt and pulled down her drawers while Tom lay there smiling. Delia began to remove her stockings and shoes when he stopped her.

"No. I wanna fuck you in your dress and everything with it." He closed his eyes. "Just like I did in Carter."

She'd forgotten she had kept her clothes on during the act then, too. About how aroused she
was while she rode with him on his carriage until he found a sleazy inn that allowed Negros. They'd gotten so hot that by the time they made it to his room, they'd both come. That's all she remembered about the very first time they fucked. How she wanted him so much she forgot about everything that led up to her satisfaction.

Delia lapped her leg over him and sank down on his dick easily. She needed no instruction or patience. She did this every day. Riding and sucking dick was like clockwork and even more instinctive with Tom because their bodies meshed together so well.

"Oh, yes." He leaned up, squeezing her generous hips as her large buttocks made a clapping sound against his skin. "Harder. Yes! Like that."

She moaned, something she rarely did when she was fucking a client. Then again, Tom wasn't a client, and he certainly wasn't just any man.

"I love your hips." He breathed. "They're so luscious."

She rode harder, her bosom bouncing.

"Like that." He grabbed her large breasts and squeezed them together, leaving an imprint on her cleavage. "Let me see your titties. I've missed them so much."

Delia's dress was already off her shoulders, so she only had to slip her dress down a bit to
unbutton the unyielding corset.

"Yes." Tom gyrated faster when he saw her breasts. "Bounce on me. Like that."

"Oh!" Delia leaned back and rubbed her fingers through her hair.

She felt like the most beautiful woman in the world.

"Turn around." Tom panted, sweat hanging off his forehead. "I wanna taste you and I want you to taste me, too."

She always enjoyed 69 the best. Nothing better than giving while receiving.

Delia turned over to where her cunt was right on his face. "You like that?"

"Yes." He gently peeled the lips apart with his fingers and licked up and down right through the center.

"Oh." Delia rocked back on his tongue.

Tom was the best lover she'd ever had. What made him stand out was how intuitive he was to a woman's body. He knew just how to lick her, to send her right to the edge but not over it.

Delia rode his tongue, grabbing at the rustling fabric of her linen dress.

"Mm." Tom gulped and munched, the sounds making Delia even hotter. "Now me, my love. Suck me."

Delia wrapped her lips around his shaft again, sucking him while he licked her.

Up and down. Down and up.

"Mm, yes!" Delia yelled as Tom rubbed his fingers across her clit. "Right there. Oh!" She looked up not knowing how long Mary-Jane had been in the doorway but there she stood.

Tom kept licking while Delia's gaze locked on his wife.

Mary-Jane ran her hands down the front of her brown and white checked gingham dress, the buttons getting in the way.

Delia went back to sucking Tom, noticing the heaving of Mary-Jane's breasts which betrayed her arousal.

Delia didn't know what to make of this. She hadn't pegged Mary-Jane as wanting a part of the action. Not the devout Christian she was.

But what did that mean? Most of the men who paid for Delia's surfaces were Christians. Or so they said.

"Mary-Jane?" Tom let Delia go.

"Don't stop." Mary-Jane pulled up her dress, showing off her black stockings. She slightly bent over and pushed her hand between her legs.

Delia gaped, not believing what she saw. Here she was afraid of being disrespectful to Mary-Jane for fornicating on the porch in the bright early morning, but Mary-Jane didn't seem to mind.

Tom went back to tasting Delia and within seconds, an orgasm shuddered from inside of her, leaving her breathless.

Mary-Jane came immediately afterwards, thanks to her hand. Then Tom followed.

Mary-Jane smiled at Delia, her cheeks turning red. "All my life, I've been the good girl. Can I have one moment when I'm not?"

Delia nodded and held her hand out to Mary-Jane.

CHAPTER FIVE

Mary-Jane lay flat in front of Delia while Tom crawled in behind Delia.

Delia caressed Mary-Jane on top of her dress to see her reaction, then when she didn't change her mind and dispute, she lifted the skirt and pulled off Mary-Jane's underwear.

Mary-Jane closed her eyes, biting her lip.

Not only was Delia great with dick, she knew her way around pussy too.

"Relax," Delia whispered to Mary-Jane. "I'm gonna make you feel good." She fingered Mary-Jane a bit before eating her out then Delia put her mouth on her, licking her clit.

"Oh." Mary-Jane writhed, her bun coming apart just from the way she was moving. "Yes, Delia." She held Delia's gyrating head, trembling uncontrollably.

Tom was busy at work fucking Delia from behind, and each stroke was more magical than the one before it. She never knew a lover like Tom who made her wetter the more they fucked.

"Ooh, yes." Delia glanced at him over her shoulder, remembering how important it was to urge the man on. "Ah!" She went back to licking Mary-Jane's soggy folds.

"Yes." Mary-Jane leaned up, moving her body with the rhythm of Delia's tongue. Without a yell or warning, she came right in Delia's face.

"Oh." Mary-Jane fell flat, stroking her hair. "Oh, God. That was incredible."

Delia licked pussy juice from her lips, proud of her skills.

"I'm coming!" Tom squeezed Delia's waist, holding her on his dick. "Ah, shit."

"Come on." Delia playfully swatted Mary-Jane's thigh. "Let's take a ride on the Tom Train."

The threesome laughed and a giddy Tom lay flat while Delia perched her pussy on his face and Mary-Jane sat on his dick.

Riding Tom's magnificent tongue, Delia couldn't take her eyes off Mary-Jane. The way she completely let loose. Hair flying, tits out, no-holds-barred. Right then, Delia knew Mary-Jane had undergone a transformation she'd never reverse. She went wild on Tom's cock, forgetting she was supposed to be the good girl and just living and enjoying herself.

Usually, wanting to cry wasn't an emotion you felt during sex, but Delia almost sobbed at how free Mary-Jane was.

She'd shed her cocoon and emerged into a beautiful butterfly.

****

Delia awoke the next morning feeling more relaxed than ever. Unlike the rickety, one-room structure she'd grown up in, The Lipnickis' home was a much sturdier and larger home with two-levels. It wasn't extravagant, but Mary-Jane had done a wonderful job at decorating to make it stand out. You could tell Tom made better money than the men around the area that relied on ranching and farming.

Delia walked down the boxed stairs. The aroma of steak and biscuits cooking in the cast iron skillets greeted her before she got to the kitchen.

Mary-Jane sat at the table, humming and knitting while she waited for breakfast to finish. Delia couldn't explain it, but she glowed. She absolutely glowed. "Good morning."

Mary-Jane looked up, a smile spreading across her naturally-pink lips. "Good morning, Delia. How are you?"

"Great." She scratched through her curls as she sat at the table. "I slept like a baby. Never sleep that well at the brothel."

"I can imagine. I slept wonderful too."

"Where's Tom?"

"He's feeding the horse." Mary-Jane knitted with precision, as if she were born to do it.

"I always wanted to knit." Delia smiled. "Momma tried to teach me, but I couldn't pick up the habit."

"It takes good concentration." Mary-Jane masterfully weaved the needle through the yawn. "Want me to teach you?"

Delia shrugged and pushed her chair beside Mary-Jane.

Mary-Jane instructed her well, but after a few clumsy attempts, Delia gave up again. "That's it." Delia laughed. "Obviously knitting is not for me."

Mary-Jane giggled. "Well, you don't need to know how to knit. You keep busier than I do."

Delia couldn't keep her and Tom's secret anymore. Not after yesterday and what they'd all shared. She liked Mary-Jane a lot and already considered the woman a friend. If she was going to keep this arrangement with the Lipnickis, Delia had to be honest.

"Mary-Jane, I need to tell you something."

She batted her eyes. "Yes?"

"Yesterday wasn't the first time Tom, and I met. We've known each other for months. We met in Carter."

Mary-Jane rested her hands on her lap.

"I'm so sorry for not being honest at first, but I didn't wanna hurt you—"

"I know, Delia."

She sat back. "What?"

"Tom told me last night after you retired, and he said he is in love with you."

Delia dropped her head, feeling like the worst person in the world. "Mary-Jane, please don't be upset."

"I'm not upset." She laughed. "I'm happier than I've ever been!"

Delia grimaced.

"If anyone should apologize, it's me to Tom for not being a better wife. After we couldn't have kids, I didn't exactly make it easy for him to love me. Then I blamed him for it. We've both done things the wrong way. I accept that."

"This isn't your fault." Delia took Mary-Jane's hand. "I'm so sorry about Tom."

"Do you love him?"

Delia dropped her head. "Yes, I do."

"I'm glad. It makes my decision much easier."

"What decision?"

"I wanna thank you so much, Delia." Mary-Jane stood, grabbing Delia up in a hug. "You've given me the greatest gift of all."

Delia hugged her back, even more confused.

"Yesterday was amazing." Mary-Jane clasped her hands. "Not just the sex, but what it meant. I came into myself, Delia. I remembered who I was and what I wanted to be." She walked around, the skirt of her dress swaying. "I haven't felt so in control of my life in years! Don't you see? If it weren't for you, I wouldn't ever have the courage to leave."

"Leave?" Delia walked across the squeaky planks. "I don't understand."

"It's a glorious day!" Mary-Jane turned in a circle with her arms out. "The best day in the world because my life starts again, and it's because of you, Delia!" Mary-Jane gave her a sisterly kiss on the cheek. "Wilkerson isn't for me anymore. I don't love Tom and he doesn't love me. I want my own life again. Tom and I have agreed to split."

"Oh my God."

"No, no." Mary-Jane waved her hands. "Don't you dare feel guilty. You're the angel we needed to wake up from this dreadful trance we'd been in. I will always care about Tom, but we do not belong together and we can't keep pretending we do."

"You're leaving?" Delia gasped. "On your own? Where are you gonna go?"

"I don't know." Mary-Jane shrugged, giggling. "I don't really care, but wherever it is, it'll be on my terms. Look, I love my faith but I can't stay here in a miserable marriage because the bible says I should. We all deserve happiness, Delia. I just didn't think I deserved it before you."

"When are you leaving?"

"Tomorrow. Tom's gonna take me to the next county and I'm gonna hitch a wagon to... wherever."

"Wow, that's fast."

Mary-Jane exhaled. "It's a long time coming. You gave me the push I needed to not be afraid to do it."

"You were so beautiful yesterday." Delia exhaled. "On the porch. It was like you were changing before my eyes. I loved seeing you cut loose and embrace your power."

"I quite enjoyed it myself." Mary-Jane giggled. "And, if I may be so bold to say, I can see why you do what you do. You're definitely good at it."

Delia winked. "I aim to please."

"Just promise me you'll love Tom with all your heart."

"I promise, I will." Delia hugged her. "Good luck on your journey, Mary-Jane. I hope you get everything you've ever wanted."

"Ooh." Mary-Jane ran to the cast iron stove to check on the food. "Everything's almost done. Could you call Tom in, please?"

As soon as Delia walked out on the porch, Tom walked up with a handful of rusty tools.

"Hello." He walked up the porch and laid the tools down. "You look even more radiant than yesterday." He kissed her. "I watched you sleep a little last night. Never saw such a treasure before in my life. Did you sleep well?"

"Mary-Jane's leaving?"

He squinted from the morning sun. "Yes."

"And how do you feel about that?"

"Confused." He crossed his arms over his lean body. "I'll miss her. She's a good woman and I

wish we'd handled things better."

Delia studied the worry lines on his face. "Do you regret her leaving?"

"No." He took her hand. "You're who I belong with, Delia. We can finally be together like we're supposed to. Mary-Jane's tougher than she looks. She'll be all right. But she has to make her path and unfortunately, it's not with me."

"That's a big step. Her leaving on her own. Most women wouldn't have the guts to do that. I

hope she finds all the happiness in the world."

"Me too." Tom hugged her. "I owe Mary-Jane the world."

Delia put her arms around him and laid her head on his slender chest. "You do?"

"Of course." He squeezed her tighter. "If it weren't for Mary-Jane, I never would've met *you*."

THE END

SAMPLE OF SEX IN KENYA: CHAPTER ONE

(2018)

"Will you stop bitching every five minutes?" Adam Jessup scrolled through his phone while he and Vette Marlon waited at the baggage carousel for their luggage. "Since we left the US, you've been complaining about everything."

"I'm hot." She fanned her face with a pamphlet, her curly yellow hair stuffed underneath her straw hat. "It's like four hundred degrees in this place. God. And why is everyone staring at us? Because we're white?"

Adam exhaled, checking the hotel reservations on his phone. "Maybe because you're being a bitch."

"Excuse me?" She moved aside as people grabbed their luggage. "You're the one with an attitude the whole time."

"That's because you complain about every damn thing." Adam stuffed his phone in his pocket. "Of course it's hot. It's Africa!"

Since he'd been a child, 30-year-old Adam's mother always told him that good people got their wish. So after all these years of living a squeaky-clean life, being an upstanding citizen and going to church even when his friends made fun of him for missing all the Sunday games, he'd finally made it to Africa.

The Global Health Foundation had sent him to Nairobi, Kenya to oversee a shipment of supplies to a local food bank. After six years of volunteering with the GHF, they'd tasked him with his first unsupervised mission and it made him damn proud.

Too bad he'd come with loud ass Vette Marlon who'd complained since they gotten off the plane. It would take a hell of a lot for Adam to hold his tongue on this trip.

They grabbed their bags from the carousel.

"This is for charity." Adam huffed as they walked toward the glass doors with people sliding in and out of them. "Think about the reason we're here."

"I don't wanna be here." Vette hurried alongside him in flip-flops. "I hate this place already. It's so hot I can't even see. Look at me, Adam." She threw out her white arm, the color of a snowstorm. "I'm paler than the average white person. I'm fuckin' translucent. You know what this sun will do to my skin? I got on five bottles of sunblock and that ain't even helping."

People gaped at Vette as she and Adam passed.

"Everyone's looking at you," Adam said. "Stop acting like a moron."

"So I'm making this up?" Her sandals clacked against the tile.

"It's not

hot to you?"

"We're from Florida, remember?" Adam huffed as they exited the airport. "You should be used to the heat... God damn." The sun punched Adam in the face as soon as they got outside. "Jesus." He slipped on his shades.

"Uh-huh." Vette folded her arms, thin mouth in a permanent scowl. "So who's complaining now?"

"Shit, my cap's in my damn luggage."

Vette grinned. "Want my hat? Sike."

"Whatever." He wiggled his toes in his Nikes. "I got on sneakers and thick socks and the sun is still burning my feet. And you got on flip-flops?" Adam looked around, noticing they seemed to be the only ones sweating and complaining. "The cement's burning through my shoes. I ain't never experienced heat like this."

"Please, *please*." Vette squeezed her hands together. "Tell me it isn't too late to go back."

"Let's find a cab, get to the hotel and out of this heat."

She saluted him. "Aye, aye, Captain!"

He mumbled, rolling his eyes.

CHAPTER TWO

If Adam expected Vette to chill once they got into the air-conditioned cab, he was wrong. She complained about the smell of the cab and that there wasn't enough room in the back to stretch her legs. But Adam refused to let these inconveniences bother him. No. He kept his mind on the sights. He tried to guess how many people there were in this little block alone, but there had to be hundreds. People walking on top of each other, in the middle of the street, through traffic. A car meant shit to them.

Brown and black ashy feet in dusty sandals. People yelling and cars honking. Bumper-to-bumper traffic. Long, ragged streets. Hustlers in old T-shirts and faded jeans looking to score off dumb tourists.

"Look at 'em." Vette took off her hat, looking around with narrow, cynical green eyes. "Like roaches."

"Shut up." Adam nudged Vette with his elbow.

The driver peeked at her from the corner of his eye.

"For some reason you thought you being in charge of this trip meant you're in charge of *me*." Vette nudged Adam back. "Well, you're not. Yeah, I said it," she yelled for the driver to hear. "They're like roaches. Walking all on top of each other. All in the streets like they don't know how to act. This isn't acceptable where we come from—"

"*Watch* it." Adam grabbed her wrist. "You don't want to sound racist do you, Vette?"

She rolled her eyes.

It wasn't that Adam was surprised. Everyone knew Vette was a racist bitch, but Adam had hoped she'd have *some* decorum for the sake of decency.

"Hey it's okay." The bright-eyed, purple-skinned driver snickered, rolling a toothpick in his mouth. "Let the lady talk. It don't bother me. She's showing her ignorance."

"Ignorance?" The imprint of Vette's bouncing breasts showed through her sweaty T-shirt. "Ain't that the pot calling the kettle black? And I mean *blacker* than *black*."

"Shut the fuck up!" Adam grabbed her arm. "I'm warning you."

"Get off me!" She struggled to free herself. "Who do you think you are?"

"I'm sorry, sir," Adam told the driver. "Believe me, I wouldn't have brought her if I didn't have to."

Vette scoffed. "No I was the only one who would come with you to this place. Let go of me, Adam." She hit him and he turned her loose.

"Is she drunk?" the driver asked.

Adam plopped back in the seat. "It's the one time she needs to be."

"A drink." Vette's eyes lit up. "That's what I need." She dug in her

purse and pulled out a tiny bottle of vodka.

Adam grabbed it before she took a swig. "What the fuck are you doing? I said no alcohol on this trip, Vette."

"Excuse me." She snatched the bottle back, batting her long lashes. "Are you my daddy? I'm twenty-eight-years-old. I can drink whenever I fucking want to."

He took the bottle again. "I'm not gonna have you sloppy drunk and acting like a fool on this trip. No drinking." He stuffed the bottle in his pocket. "You settle down."

She crossed her arms, smacking her lips.

"We're gonna go to the hotel, refresh, get to the food bank and help with the shipment. Drop the attitude, Vette. I'm warning you."

"Eat me, Adam." She squinted. "Oh, I forgot. You already did."

The driver chuckled.

Adam groaned. "Bitch."

****

"Thank God we're here!" Vette plopped down on Adam's hotel bed. "I'm glad we got rooms right next to each other. Ah." She kicked off her shoes. "I'm drained. That flight took everything out of me."

Whenever the GHF sent volunteers on overseas assignments, they always paid for the rooms and while Adam had been stuck in some dumps before, the Foundation didn't do too shabby this time.

A multi-room suite wrapped in subtle, yellow lighting brought charm to the dreary brown walls. Sand-colored curtains made the space cozier while the chic furniture stayed true to the room's swanky integrity.

"This is pretty nice, huh?" Adam opened the intricate wooden doors of the balcony, greeted by the sticky humidity.

"Are you crazy?" Vette scoffed. "I'm dying to get out of the heat and you're going back into it?"

Adam rested on the aluminum railing, admiring the city across the horizon. "You can see everything from here. Wow, look at that pool. It's huge."

"I'll pass."

"Come on, Vette. Compared to the places the GHF has put us in, you gotta admit this is beautiful."

"It should be with all the work we do for them and for *free*, I might add."

Adam expected to find a hotel like this in ritzy Florida spots like Boca Grande or Naples, not tucked away in a quiet corner away from the rest of Nairobi.

"Did you see how the guy at the front desk was looking at us?" Vette asked.

Adam chuckled. "Everyone's been looking at us."

"Yeah, well." Vette stood, rubbing the bedspread. "I don't like it. Make sure you lock up your stuff. They'll come in our rooms and rob us blind."

"Why?" Adam scratched his arm. "Neither of us have shit. We're broker than two jokes."

"You know how they are."

He looked back at her. "Do me a favor? While we're here, keep your racist comments to yourself because I don't appreciate them."

"Racist? Come on, you've heard how they are here in Africa."

"How are *they*?"

"Please. You can be Mr. Woke all you want to, but it's just us now. Why do you think everyone warned us about the crime in this place? They didn't just make it up."

"And there's not crime in Florida?"

"Yes, there's definitely crime in Florida and look who's committing it." She stretched. "I was born in Tallahassee, and I barely recognize it now. Every sign's in Mexican. The neiGHForhoods are a mess. It wasn't like that before—"

"I don't wanna hear this shit."

"Look at California. The Mexicans took over, and it's a dump."

"Why are you even a part of the GHF with the way you are? You do realize many who need our help are not white?"

"Don't give me that. You know how they all are."

"*Who?*" he shouted.

"The blacks, the Mexicans, Muslims, name them."

"Get the fuck out of my room."

"I'm not trying to fight with you—"

"Go!" He pointed at the door. "Don't make me throw you out."

"Fine." She snatched her purse, swung it over her shoulder and twisted to the door. "I'll be in my room if you need me."

Adam rolled his eyes as he turned back to the balcony. "I won't."

"You won't? Are you sure about that?"

"More than sure, Vette." He kept his back to her, enraptured by the aroma of fruit and spices from the street markets.

"Hmm." She joined him on the balcony and stood right behind him. "You're lying." She walked her delicate fingers down his sweaty nape. "Remember our night, Adam? After the GHF Christmas party last year?"

He sighed, flinching at her touch.

"We had a moment, wouldn't you say?" She hugged him from behind. "I bet you hadn't felt that good in a long time. Remember, how upset you were that night because your wife left you? I was there, Adam." She lay against his back, squeezing his abs. "I was there when you had no one else."

CHAPTER THREE

"Vette." Adam pulled at her hands. "Leave."

"Why are you treating me this way?" she purred. "So mean and hateful with the things you say?"

"Oh, I'm not the one with the problem here." He pushed her away and faced her. "And let's not talk about who's mean and hateful."

"You enjoyed that night." She pushed curls out of her face. "You said you did."

"We were *drunk*. It was just one night when things got out of hand."

"*No*." She sucked her lip. "You wanted me. You can't deny the attraction." She tangled her fingers in his T-shirt. "Why would you want to?"

"I told you." He pushed her again. "It was a mistake. I don't have feelings for you, Vette."

"Yeah?" She lowered her stare to his crotch. "If I stayed in here long enough, you would."

"Out." He shoved her, causing her to stumble. "Go refresh or whatever so we can get to the food bank and do what they need us to do. That's why we came here, remember?"

"Fuck you." She sashayed off the balcony and grabbed her purse. "I got better things to do then hang around your stuck up ass all day."

"What?" He hurried into the room. "We're supposed to help the food bank—"

"You're so perfect and in charge, you do it."

"We have a job to do here. Why the fuck did you even sign up for this trip if you didn't want to help?"

"You're so smart, right?" She opened the door. "Guess." She left.

"Jesus." Adam shook off his frustration, because there were more important things to think about than Vette, and as he unpacked, someone knocked on his door.

"Mr. Adam?" a man beckoned with a high-pitched East African accent.

Adam recognized the voice of the front desk manager, Meshack, and answered the door. "Hello."

The giddy, yellow-skinned African with freckles dotting his face, grinned back from ear-to-ear. "Hello, Mr. Adam. I wanted to make sure you're settling in all right. Is the room sufficient for you?"

"Oh, yes it's lovely." Adam smiled, holding his waist. "Thank you. What can I do for you?"

"Well..." Meshack's sparse eyebrows danced. "It's more of what I can do for *you*." He held a lopsided grin as he raised on his tiptoes to peek over Adam's shoulder. "Is your uh, companion with you?"

"Companion?" Adam grimaced. "You mean Vette? No, she went to her room, I guess."

"Excuse me if I am prying, but are you not together?"

"Hell no." Adam shook his head. "No, no way."

"I can be of help to you then." The much-shorter man strutted inside, his name badge sitting crooked on his flabby chest. "I didn't want to share this in front of your lady friend, but we offer special 'amenities' for the gentlemen at the hotel if they're interested."

Adam squinted, closing the door. "Special amenities?"

"You know." Meshack leaned forward, eyebrow raised. "We like to make our guests' stay as pleasurable as possible."

"Ah." Adam snickered. "You're one of those hotels that hire out prostitutes for tourists?"

"Not prostitutes. *Escorts*. It goes beyond sex. She will show you around the city and spend time with you. We deal with a company and everything is safe and reputable." Meshack told Adam the name of the company. "The women are gorgeous, clean and STD-free."

Adam scratched the back of his head. "That's not really my thing—"

"Sometimes you don't know what your thing is until you try it." Meshack winked. "This is a professional service, the women are of age, they get paid fairly and are treated very well." He twisted his face. "No trafficking, drugs or abuse, no. I'd never condone anything like that. You just get the company of a beautiful woman to help you pass the time." He smiled. "Surely, you can't say no to *that*."

CHAPTER FOUR

Adam checked in with the food bank and got back to the hotel by nightfall. He stopped at Vette's room, but she didn't answer. Either she'd left or was ignoring him and though he regretted throwing her out of his room earlier, he was too exhausted for her bullshit.

Drained, Adam headed to bed when someone knocked on his door around 9 PM. He greeted a stunning African woman with a purse on her arm and a large basketful of towels, soaps, and lotions.

The escort.

Shit. He'd forgotten about her.

She smiled with the whitest teeth he'd ever seen. Cinnamon-brown eyes sparkled against her rich, chestnut-brown skin.

She slipped inside the room smelling of coconut.

Adam was 6'2 so according to where her head hit him she was at least 5'9. God had blessed her with elegant, narrow features that enthralled a man on the spot.

She sashayed to the dresser, the multicolored wrap dress massaging her sleek, thin frame. She turned and smiled at Adam. "Hujambo," which meant, "hello" in Swahili. "My name is Grace Gitau. It's nice to meet you, Mr. Jessup. I hope you are enjoying your stay in Nairobi so far."

Grace?

Adam expected some exotic African name. "Thank you." He cleared his

throat. "Nairobi's lovelier than I could imagine."

And so are you.

"This might sound stupid." He chuckled. "But I'm guessing you're the escort?"

Her tiny, triangular-shaped breasts jiggled underneath the sheer material. "Yes."

36

"Okay." He exhaled, rocking. "I've never done this before."

"I understand."

His loins melted at the sound of her sultry accent. "Forgive me if I'm a little nervous."

"You've been with ladies before, haven't you?"

"Of course."

She blinked. "This is no different."

"I disagree." Adam chuckled, rubbing his hair. "I've never been with a complete stranger."

"That's what makes this easier." She wiggled her shoulders. Everything she did spelled sex.

"Emotions get in the way." She smiled. "Sometimes it's best to let your mind rest and have your body take control."

He nodded. "Guess I never thought of it as so straightforward."

"It can be." Grace took off her head wrap showing him her braids in a pristine bun and then her phone rang, destroying the intimacy. "Excuse me." She rushed to the dresser and grimaced as she got her cell out of her purse. "It is nothing." She sighed. "Sorry about that."

"Everything's okay?"

"Yes." She fidgeted as she put her phone away. "What were we talking about?"

"About this uh... arrangement." Adam chuckled. "It's new to me and all."

Her phone rang again.

She huffed as she yanked the phone out again. "I apologize."

"No, it's no problem. If you need to take that I can wait—"

"No." She stabbed her finger into the phone. "I will turn it on vibrate."

"You sure everything is okay?"

"Just an overzealous client." She flashed a forced smile as she sat on the bed. "Just ignore it if it buzzes. You're enjoying the city?"

"Yes."

"What do you like about it so far?"

"Well…" Sweat beaded on the back of Adam's neck, but it wasn't from the heat. "I haven't seen any sights yet, but I like the hotel and the food is amazing. Meshack said you can show me around the city?"

"I'd love to." She looked up at him through her flirty lashes. "I'm here to make your trip as pleasurable as possible. You've paid for a good time and I plan to give it to you."

Like any other business deal, Grace showed him her ID, proving her age of twenty-eight and even presented a document showing she was healthy and free of any disease. She spelled out the rules. No kissing on the lips, no weird or outrageous sex acts, and no action without use protection. If he didn't agree, no deal.

"I'm confused," Adam said. "Why does the company not allow kisses?"

"It's not *them*, Mr. Jessup." She put the document back into her purse. "The kissing is *my* rule. I don't allow my clients to kiss me on the lips."

"Why not?"

"Because kissing is too personal."

"Hold on." He laughed. "You can have intercourse with random men but they can't kiss you?"

"These are the rules." She shrugged one shoulder. "If you don't agree I will leave."

"No, it's just I don't see why kissing is different from everything else."

"It's just a line I won't cross."

"What if I forget? I mean, when we're into it? What if I do it by accident?"

"You won't."

"How do you know?"

Her mouth rose in the corner as she smiled. "I'll remind you."

He didn't like this. Didn't like it at all. Adam loved kissing. It was his favorite part of having sex.

Shit, he paid for her, he should be able to kiss her if he wanted.

He'd accept it because the last thing he wanted was Grace leaving. And though he didn't like this no-kissing shit one bit, he would savor every moment with this African goddess. Kiss or not, she'd been the woman of his dreams before he knew she existed.

CHAPTER FIVE

Grace removed her dress and glided to Adam buck-naked with no qualms at all and unbuttoned his shirt. His heart flip-flopped like it did when that sexy doctor gave him that penis exam a few years back when he had that savage urinary tract infection.

Grace moved like a robot, undressing him without batting an eye. Her mind trained on the mission. She was the escort, but Adam worried about pleasing *her*. He was no nervous he couldn't imagine getting into his groove. What if he were so bad she canceled the arrangement and gave him a refund? Talk about embarrassing.

"Relax." She smiled.

"Have you ever been with a woman?" he blurted out, not knowing why the hell he had.

She wiggled her dainty nose. "No."

"Did I offend you?"

She laughed. "Why would I be offended?" She threw his shirt on the floor. "You'd be shocked what clients ask me." She bent down, yanking at his zipper.

"*Whoa.*" He jerked, chuckling. "You don't waste time, do you?"

Her stiff, black nipples jiggled as she removed his pants.

"You said you get a lot of weird questions from clients?"

"It comes with the territory." She stood upright. "Some think that because I'm an escort, I have no boundaries. You won't believe what some people want me to do." She held her waist, perky breasts standing at attention. "There's some very freaky people out here."

Adam clenched his dick through his underwear, imagining how her mouth would feel on it. "Anyone ever get rough with you?"

"Some have tried, but I can handle myself."

He stared at her nipples, looking like giant Hershey's Kisses.

"Sit down," she commanded.

Adam sat, and she bent down in front of him, snatching off his socks.

Here he was sitting in front of her with this big, swollen pink cock ajar in her face and she looked at it like a secretary filing papers. Of course this was a job to her, but Adam expected a smile, a moan, any acknowledgement of his blessed member. After all, this cock had sent his soon-to-be ex-wife into fits of infinite ecstasy, but Grace's aloof reaction made him wonder just how many men she'd fucked.

She fluttered her long lashes. "We're going to take a shower."

"Huh?"

"Come on." She grabbed the basket and went to the bathroom.

By the time Adam got in there she was already under the water, standing against the tile wall, staring at him. "Get in."

He swallowed, even the creases in the bend of his knees sweated.

Oh, make no mistake. He wanted to fuck her. Wanted to beat the brakes off that sweet, African punani but paying for it just felt desperate and awkward. And it didn't help that Grace looked at his dick like a scientist in a laboratory.

"You ever had sex in the shower?" she asked.

"I've had sex in lots of places."

"Ah." She raised an eyebrow. "Get a lot of women?"

"Can't complain."

He wasn't cocky but he'd never met a woman who didn't find him

attractive. So he'd never had a problem finding fuck partners and though he'd been faithful to his wife, he'd been surprised at how many women didn't give a damn he was married and tried to get a spin on his old "love rod" anyway.

Grace tilted her head. "You're a ladies man?"

"I wouldn't say *that*. I mean I don't do nothing for it to happen. Women just like me."

She grinned. "I see."

"I'm not trying to be arrogant." He chuckled, waving off his last statement. "But it's true. Just something about me I guess."

"There definitely is." Grace's stare showered his body. "You are a beautiful man, Adam. Coal-black hair and killer blue eyes. Great body."

He tingled, clearing his throat. "Thank you." He stepped under the water and grinned as the warm sprinkles tickled his nipples.

"I bet your father is so handsome," Grace said.

"I wouldn't know."

She gaped.

"Never met the man or seen one picture." He scratched his arm. "Apparently he was just some dude my mom banged after meeting him in a bar."

"I'm sorry."

"It's okay. You don't miss what you never had."

"You don't know anything about him?"

"Mom stayed tightlipped but I have heard rumors through the years that he was married when they hooked up. Either way he doesn't want nothing to do with me."

She stuck out her chin. "How do *you* know?"

"I figure if he wanted to know me he'd been around."

"But you don't know if he tried to be around you. You have no idea what happened between him and your mother. Maybe he wanted to be in your life but your mother didn't want him to be."

He shook his head. "No, no."

"How do you *know*, Adam?" She clasped his wrist. "If your mother never said the reason and you've never met the man, you're just guessing." She let him go. "Don't judge your father when you can't be sure of what's going on."

"You're right. I don't know but still, if any woman tried to keep me from my kid, I'd do all I could to see him. So that's why I think he's full of shit. Sorry I just do. Can we talk about something else?"

"Like your penis?" She chuckled as she reached out the shower and got a rag from the basket. "I like it." Grace flung him around and washed his back and shoulders.

As if he wasn't nervous enough, he got an intense cramp in the pit of his stomach and cursed himself for having that steak and onions for dinner.

Shit. Please don't fart.

He held it in until the pain subsided and his ass relaxed.

Thank God.

If he'd farted, he might've blown poor Grace back into the hallway.

"You're so tense." She kneeled while working the rag up his thighs, the aromatic soap scenting the bathroom.

She washed between his wet cheeks, massaging his asshole, his dick about to pop.

"Mm." He grabbed it with both hands.

She snickered. "Feel good?"

"Yeah." He wiggled his toes in the water. "You need to bathe me more often."

She smiled. "There you go. You're relaxing. Hold on because the fun's just beginning. Turn around."

He did, and she washed his abdomen, dragging the rag through his thick, black pubic hair.

He glared down at her, talking to her with his eyes.

Get the tip. Please, please get the tip.

She finished washing or *teasing* him and smiled. "Your turn."

"Uh, okay." Adam got a new rag out the basket.

Grace turned around and pressed her hands to the wet tile, tight little brown ass shining with water. "Take your time."

Adam glided the rag over her glossy skin, exploring every inch of her.

The shifting muscles in her back. The curve of her bony hips, the smooth, never-ending length of her creamy legs.

"How did you get into escorting?"

She glanced at him over her skinny shoulder. "Kind of personal, you think?"

"We're two strangers sharing a shower." He grinned as he turned her around, looking right into her delicious nipples. "I think we're passed subtleties."

"Just circumstances, I guess." She pursed her pouty lips, creases running through her forehead. "There aren't many options around here especially for women. You do what you need to, to survive."

"I don't buy that." He massaged her arm with the rag. "You seem like a resourceful woman. There's gotta be more you can do than this."

She raised her eyebrows. "Are you saying you have an issue with my line of work?"

"I can't complain about any occupation that puts a beautiful woman in my shower unless you're not being treated right. I hope that's not the case."

"The company I work for? Oh, no it's wonderful. Very professional place. I'm not forced to do anything I don't want. It's just like any other job. We sign contracts and are held to high standards and we even get bonuses."

"Bonuses, huh?" He pinched her cheek. "What do you have to do for these bonuses?"

She wriggled, coyly. "I'm not being abused and I can walk away at any time. I choose to do this because compared to anything else, it's one of the best ways I can make money fast to help my family. Besides, if I wasn't an escort, we'd never met."

He smirked, squeezing out the rag.

"You're different. Clients usually don't care about my life. They just get what they want and go."

"Well, I'm not like that."

"Why are you here again?"

"In Kenya?" He licked his lips as he moved the rag over her kinky pussy hairs. "I'm a volunteer with the Global Health Foundation. They sent me to check the shipment for the food bank and help them get things organized."

"That's wonderful. How did you get into that?"

"Well, my mom always instilled in me how important it is to be a good person." He fondled her pussy through the rag. "That there is always someone out there that needs a hand, and I like helping people."

"I want to move to the States. I'm working toward my Visa."

"That's great."

"Where are you from?"

"Tallahassee, Florida."

"Really?" She gushed. "I have family in Miami."

"Wow, it is a small world, huh?"

"Do you travel a lot with the Foundation?"

"I've been all over the world, but it feels different this time."

"Why?"

"I don't know." His temperature rose as he looked into her soothing eyes. "Maybe it's the company."

She smiled and after he finished washing her, she went back to work on him, stroking and teasing.

Adam struggled not to climax, but Grace just wouldn't leave his cock alone.

"Ooh." He wobbled, holding the wall. "I'm coming."

"Yes, Adam." She rubbed faster, pointing his dick to her tits. "Come now. Give it to me. I want it so bad."

"Oh. Ah!" He ejaculated, squirting thick cream right on her chest. "Ooh. Fuck."

Grace moaned, cum hanging from her nipples. "Good *boy*."

CHAPTER SIX

"Lay down," Grace ordered Adam once they got back into the bedroom. "Put your face into the pillow."

"What are we doing?"

"Trust me. You will like it."

Adam melted every time Grace touched him, and this time was no different. He breathed into the lavender-scented pillow as she massaged him, calming every muscle. His loins raced, dick swelling into another erection.

She climbed her damp, thin body onto his back and rubbed her furry pussy against the crease in his back.

"Hmm." Adam wiggled his toes, feeling as if he were floating on air. "This is *amazing*."

She leaned down, whispering into his ear. "It gets better."

He held his breath, nearly busting a nut on the sheet.

"Roll over."

He did, and she got on top of him again, massaging his chest while rolling her pussy against his cock.

"You like this?" She held a mischievous smile that told him she already knew he did.

"Fuck, yeah." He wiggled his erection against her. "Don't ever have to ask."

"It feels like..." She bounced, sending sharp sensations through his shaft. "You wanna fuck. Do you?"

"Again, you don't have to ask." He grinded against her moist labia but didn't enter. "I've wanted to fuck you since I saw you."

She blushed. "Do you like this position or something else?"

He loved that view of looking up at a woman's tits as she bounced on his dick, but he wanted to see that ass.

"Turn around." He narrowed his eyes. "Ride it from the other direction."

"Okay—"

"And take your hair down."

He loved pulling a woman's hair when he fucked her.

"Your wish is my command." She unwrapped her braids from the bun and flipped them over one shoulder.

"Yeah." He swallowed. "You are so beautiful."

She turned around, spread her ass cheeks apart with her hands and

sat on his dick.

"*Yes.*" Adam wrapped his hands into her braids. "That's it. Ride me, Grace."

"With pleasure—"

Her purse buzzed.

"Fuck." Adam groaned. "Your phone again."

"I...I apologize." She climbed off him and got her purse. "Sorry." Adam sighed, scratching his balls.

"You've got to be kidding me." She read the screen. "Ten times?"

"What? Is that the same person from earlier?"

"I'm turning it off." She pressed her fingertip into the phone. "It's nothing."

"Doesn't seem like nothing. Is someone bothering you, Grace?"

"No, no." She got a condom from the basket and twisted back to the bed. "Please forget it."

"You keep walking like *that* and it'll be easy to. I love the way you walk."

She giggled, and it was the first time he noticed her dimples.

"Seriously," he said. "You can tell me if you need help."

"I'm fine, Adam. It's not your concern."

"You said it was a client earlier—"

"Please." She slipped the condom on him. "Don't ruin the mood."

"Okay." He took her hand. "Lay down."

"I thought you wanted me on top."

"Not anymore." He laid her down beside him and while stroking her braids, lost himself in her intoxicating eyes and attempted a kiss.

"No." She frowned, lifting her finger between their mouths.

Fuck it, he worked on her titty, sucking and flicking the nipple back and forth with his tongue. Sensing she was ready for him, he fondled her pussy and spread her sticky labia open.

Grace panted, catching her breath in her throat.

"Fuck foreplay." He rolled her over, mounted her and shoved his pulsating dick inside her.

She thrashed against him, grabbing at the sheets and moaning.

Her cunt made him feel like a starved, desperate dope feign who'd finally gotten his fix after stumbling around for days searching for a high. Every thrust introduced his dick to a unique sensation.

He thought his soon-to-be ex-wife Ronnie had been the best fuck he had, with drunk ass Vette a close second, but they didn't compare to Grace one bit.

"Right there, Grace." He squeezed his fingers into her soft flesh. "Oh."

Adam humped harder, the bed frame beating the wall like it was Floyd Mayweather. "Whose pussy is this, huh? Whose is it?"

"Yours."

"Who? Say my name." He yanked her braids. "Say my fucking name."

"It's yours, Adam!"

"You damn right it is." He moved faster, riding that cunt like a beast. "Say my name again. Loud!"

"Adam, yes!" She grabbed his arms, her titties bouncing from side-to-side. "Oh! Don't stop."

****

"No."

Adam awoke the next morning to Grace arguing in his bathroom. It took him a second to realize she was on the phone.

"I mean it," she said. "Leave me alone. I can't take this anymore."

Adam heard her heading out the bathroom and lay over, pretending he was still asleep. "Oh." He pretended to awake when she entered. "Hey there."

"Good morning, Adam." She glided to the bed in her dress, looking like a living portrait. "Did you sleep well?"

"The best sleep I've had in years." He stretched against the fluffy pillows. "You're dressed. Are you leaving? You promised to show me around the city today."

"I'd love to." Her white teeth gleamed. "And I shall. I have to run to my place to freshen up and then I'll be back." She gestured to her dress, grinning. "I don't want to go out in the same dress as last night."

"Why not?" He took her hand and pulled her on the bed. "You look gorgeous in it. You look even better out of it."

She set her cellphone on the nightstand.

"Let me guess. Was that the same person who called you all last night?"

"Sh." She pressed her finger to his lips.

"Mm." He put his arm around her waist. "Let me kiss you—"

"No." She jerked back. "No, Adam."

"In this moment, looking into my eyes and being this close, you're telling me you don't want to kiss me?" He inched his mouth to hers. "Come on—"

"Adam, I will leave." She pressed her lips together. "These are my rules. If you can't accept them—"

"Fine." He let her go, mumbling.

"Don't be mad." She stroked his cheek. "After this, you won't even think about a kiss." She got another condom and within moments, Grace had him hard as cement, riding his stick with animalistic fervor.

"Ah, yeah." Adam gripped her waist, bouncing her. "Yes, Grace." He pushed his back into the bed. "Yes."

The bed shrieked and squealed, shaking the nightstand off balance.

"I love your dick, Adam." She bounced harder. "You're so handsome."

He grunted. "Slow it down a bit. Ah."

If Grace's pussy had a name, it would've been "magic".

She spun her hips, gyrating and thrusting until he flooded the condom.

"Ahhhh." Adam jiggled her, draining every drop of cum into the rubber.

"Oh." She rolled over breathless, her brown body dotted in sweat. "You're so good."

He rubbed his sweaty abs. "Am I?"

"Oh, *yes.*" She closed her eyes, her entire body trembling as she exhaled. "Many of my clients are horrible because they don't care about pleasing me and only getting off. But you please me, Adam."

"If you don't enjoy it then I won't." He kissed her hand. "I'm jealous."

"Jealous?"

"Of that client who keeps calling you. Guess he's hooked, huh? Can't blame him. I'm hooked now too."

"Adam." She leaned up. "You are getting confused."

"I'm not confused." He dragged his finger down her thigh. "I know exactly what I'm saying."

"I'm an escort, Adam." She swallowed. "This is just business."

"If you stay here long enough..." He held her neck, guiding her mouth to his. "It can be more—"

"No." She shook her head, pushing him away. "Please, stop, Adam."

"*Why?*" He let her go. "Why can you fuck me, bathe me, but I can't get a kiss?"

She avoided eye contact. "This is a job."

"Bullshit. How we talk, what we've shared, it's more than business."

"After one night?"

"Yes after one fuckin' night. I feel something for you, Grace. Already."

"I'll have sex with you anytime you want. Make your stay pleasurable, but we can't cross that line." She tightened her lips. "No kissing."

"Fuck that." Adam grabbed her again. He never manhandled women, but he needed to kiss her if only to make her realize this was more than a job. Or maybe convince himself it was. "Come here." He grabbed her skinny face.

"No!" She fidgeted, whimpering and shoving. "Stop it."

He let her go and slammed his head against the pillow.

"You want me to leave and not come back? Because you're acting like an animal."

He sighed into his hands.

"You say you're different than my other clients but you're acting just like them." She stood. "Like just because you pay for my time you own me. Well, you do not." She twisted to the dresser and got her ponytail holder. "I will not be disrespected."

"Fuck, Grace, I'm human. I *want* to kiss you. I'm not apologizing for that."

"What is it with you men? What women say isn't important?"

"I didn't say that."

"I don't belong to you or any man." She wrapped the ponytail holder around her hair and twisted her braids into a bun. "I am tired of men thinking they can take anything they want from me. Tired, Adam."

"All right calm down. Jeez." He straightened the pillow behind his head. "I won't do it again."

"You better not." She got her phone from the nightstand. "Or money or not, this is over."

CHAPTER SEVEN

"Hello, Grace." Sokoro Otieno greeted her when she entered her home, his voice so deep it shook the octagon tiles of her living room.

"What is this?" She yanked her key out her door before closing it. "Sokoro, what are you doing in my house?"

The 32-year-old lothario remained on her white sectional, his 6'5 body tucked into jeans and a white Gucci blazer, gold jewelry glistening from his silky, cocoa-brown skin. "I'm tired of you ignoring me."

She threw her purse on the glass coffee table. "Get out of my house or I'll call the law."

"The law?" He laughed, his perfect square teeth so white they could light up the darkness. "You forget who I am, Grace? I own the law. Everyone around here does what I say and you will be no different."

"Why are you doing this? Please, leave me alone."

"You weren't telling me to leave you alone after I gave your family that one million shillings when the white man tried to force your family off their land, were you?" He rubbed his slick, bald head, angular cheeks flexing with every word he spoke. "Weren't telling me to go away when your family needed money for food or when your mother got sick and couldn't afford her medication. What's changed?"

"We didn't know we'd made a deal with the devil."

"You should've known." He lifted his athletic frame off the couch, closing his blazer. "You refuse me, Grace? I'm royalty around here. I got women throwing themselves at my feet—"

"Then harass *them*. I won't nothing to do with you, Sokoro. Leave me and my family alone or you will be sorry."

His cackle rattled through her, shaking the walls. "Oh, that's what I love about you, Grace. Your spunk. Not that your beauty isn't more than enough to keep a man satisfied and your uh..." He walked his stare down her body. "Your other attributes. Should I mention them?"

"You'll never have me, Sokoro."

"Is that, right? Oh, wait. I had you already." He winked. "More than once. Did you forget?"

"You had my body." She stuck her chin in the air. "Not my heart. That you'll never get no matter how much money you have or how many times you threaten my family."

"I wouldn't be so sure." He straightened his sleeve. "Either your family pays the debt they owe for me saving that godforsaken dump of a village, or you marry me." His wide smile took up his entire face. "Simple as that."

"Never!"

"Come on, Grace. Let me make an honest woman out of you. You can't like slinging your body to every tourist that comes into town."

"I'd rather fuck every scoundrel on this earth than to be with you. You don't even need the money, Sokoro. You do this to torture us. To show you're in control."

"So because I'm well off, I don't deserve my money back?" He shook his head, clicking his jaw. "What world are you living in, Grace? You expect thousands for free and me get nothing? I'm not even asking for all the other times your sniveling joke of a father came begging me for money."

"Stop it." She got on her tiptoes but didn't reach anywhere close to his face. "My father is an honorable man. Ten times the man you'll ever be."

"So honorable he can't even support his family? Living in that pigsty village? Is that what you want to go back to, Grace?" He frowned. "The bush? Bathing with the same animals you eat? Drinking their feces? You want to live like an animal?"

"Don't you ever talk about my family that way. We are proud people!"

"So proud that your parents pimp their daughter out for money?"

She raised her hand to slap him, but he grabbed it.

"Uh-uh." He squinted his espresso-brown eyes. "You'd better think about that real quick, Sweetheart. Let's not get violent, Grace. You won't win that fight."

"Let me go!" She snatched her hand free.

"Marry me."

"You don't have to force a woman into marriage." She rubbed her aching wrist. "You're gorgeous and rich. You could have any woman you want."

"And I want *you*. Why is that so hard for you to understand?"

She rocked. "I'll get you the money myself."

He laughed. "You gonna suck every dick in Nairobi? Because that's what it will take for you to raise what your family owes me. You're doing well for yourself Grace, but not *that* well." He walked around her living room of slate-blue walls and icy-gray tile floor. "This is a beautiful home, but we know it wasn't easy for the village girl to come up. How do you think you rented this place, Grace?"

"With the money I make." She grimaced. "How the fuck do you think?"

"You have no credit." He walked behind the couch, massaging the back of it as he did. "Even with what you make, how do you think you got a deal on a place like this in this neiGHForhood?"

She held her breath.

"Me, Grace." He walked across the rug to the connecting kitchen. "I got this place for you."

"Liar! I bought this with *my* money."

"Because I spoke to the owner."

She shook, gritting her teeth. "You're lying."

"Course he's no longer the owner." He got the carton of orange juice out of the refrigerator.

"What are you talking about?"

Sokoro stared at her as he drank. "Ah." He set the glass on the counter. "I own this house now. I bought it last week. Hello, Grace." He grinned. "Meet your new landlord."

"Filthy liar. You're lying to manipulate me."

"It is true." He walked out the kitchen, approaching her. "You can't get away from me, Grace. I own you just like I do this property. Now..." He caressed her shoulders as she fought not to vomit. "You can be a smart girl and realize all a life with me offers or you can go back to the bush and bathe with the rhinos. Of course, if your family doesn't repay me, your village will be gone and your family dead—"

"Sokoro." She covered her mouth, gasping. "Please leave my family alone. I beg you."

"Oh, Grace." He took off her head wrap and pushed his nose into her braids. "That's the deal. You do what I want or suffer the consequences."

"No." She punched his chest as he strangled her in his embrace. "I'll get you the money. Leave my family alone!"

"You'll get me the money?"

"Yes." She sobbed. "Yes!"

"Okay." He pulled her head back. "But I need some collateral." He unbuckled his belt with his free hand.

"No." She squeezed her eyes shut. "No, Sokoro."

"Sh." He lowered her on her knees as she trembled. "Be a good girl, Grace. Show your appreciation for all I've done."

"No, please." He held her head still as he unzipped his pants. "No!"

CHAPTER EIGHT

"Trust me, Adam." Grace accompanied Adam from his hotel room a few hours later. "I'll show you all Nairobi can offer."

"Sounds great but are you all right? You seem like something is on your mind."

"I'm fine." She smiled, yet Adam wasn't convinced. "We'll go everywhere. Let me see." Her eyes lit up as she clasped her hands, bracelets jiggling. "You like animals?"

"I love animals."

"Great. We'll go to the National Park and the Safari Walk."

"Sounds nice." He didn't care if they visited a dump as long as he could spend the day with Grace.

They walked downstairs. Grace's dress brushed the steps as her sandals held her delicate feet. "We'll go to the Karen Blixen Museum too. You'll love it!"

"Who is Karen Blixen?"

"*Adam.*" She groaned and even that sounded sexy. "Karen Blixen is the author of *Out of Africa.* Remember the movie with Meryl Streep and Robert Redford?"

"I remember the movie but didn't know it was a book." He laughed as they got to the first floor.

"The book is even better than the movie. It's the story of Karen's life in Africa." She stuck her skinny finger in the air. "You should read it. I'm a true romantic and that book blew me away."

"*You* blow me away."

Grace dipped her head, redness caressing her brown cheeks. "You are sweet."

"And you're amazing."

"Ah, Mr. Adam." Meshack rocked behind the front desk with a smile as wide as Canada. "Good day. Did you sleep well?"

"Very well." Adam stood at the counter, winking at Grace, who rolled her eyes with a snicker. "Everything's perfect."

"Well, I'm glad to hear that," Meshack said. "Grace is a sweetie and tourists love her. She knows the city well and will take care of you."

"I will." She batted her sweeping lashes.

Adam rubbed up against her. "And I want to be taken care *of*."

"Well, well, well," Vette walked down the stairs. "What do we have here?" She stopped in front of Grace and Adam with resting bitch face. "And you are?"

"I'm Grace." Grace bowed, holding her hand out to her. "It's nice to meet you."

Vette glared at her hand and then at Adam. "And where did he find you?"

Grace grimaced, pulling her hand back. "He didn't *find* me anywhere."

"Grace is a tour guide." Adam took Grace's arm. "I found her on the Internet. She's gonna show me around the city."

"Do I look stupid to you?" Vette crossed her arms. "If she's a tour guide than I'm your mother."

"Then we'll be seeing you, 'Mom'." Adam rolled his eyes as he pulled Grace away toward the door. "We have things to do."

"So I'm not invited?" Vette scoffed.

"I invited you to see the sights yesterday. You didn't want to." Adam opened the door for Grace. "After you."

"You're just leaving me here?" Vette yelled. "What the fuck am I supposed to do?"

A passing woman gasped at the vulgarity.

"You're a resourceful woman, Vette." Adam winked. "I'm sure you'll find some way to entertain yourself." He helped Grace out the door.

"Who was that?" Grace asked as they exited the front steps.

"Nobody."

She faced him, fixing her purse on her shoulder. "She likes you."

He nodded, taking a stick of gum from his pocket. "How do you know?"

"I'm a woman." She patted his cheek. "We know *everything*."

CHAPTER NINE

Grace promised Adam a hell of a time and she did not disappoint. She showed Adam places he'd never heard of and the more Adam saw, the more curious he got. His heart warmed at every stop and he could feel why they called Africa "The Motherland". It wasn't just for black heritage, but Africa had lent so much of its beauty and authenticity to the American way of life that it was impossible for Adam not to be thankful.

After touring Ngong Hills, Grace took Adam to a two-story restaurant made of bamboo walls and decorated with East African artifacts. Striking waitresses strutted around in vibrant, multi-colored head wraps that matched their dresses.

Adam and Grace got an outside table where they could see the overlapping mountains in the distance.

Nairobi was unlike any place Adam had been because every experience was a part of its culture. The aroma of curry powder and strong native spices tickled his nose. The restaurant alone told Adam everything he needed to know about the city.

Grace ordered them beef curry along with her favorite and a very common Kenyan dish; Ugali, a porridge made of maize flour.

Food looked like a painting on the plates; bright, lively and rich with a variety of heat and spices which made Adam feel like he tasted African culture with each bite.

"You said this was super food." Adam chewed. "What makes it super?"

Grace sipped from her glass of apple juice with a straw. "Because it's my favorite."

He laughed. "That makes sense."

"Why? Do you not like it?"

"No, I love it. It's delicious. I love the spices. Don't tell my mom, but this is the best cooking I've ever had."

Grace smiled while chewing. "I grew up on this food."

"Are you a good cook?"

"Of course." She bounced, sitting back. "All Nairobi women can cook. It is a big part of our culture. Cooking is how we show love to our family. You should taste my cooking."

Adam rubbed the toe of his sneaker against her leg. "There's something else of yours I'd love to taste."

"I'm serious." She chuckled, swatting his foot away. "You should let me cook for you."

"I'd love that but might not have enough time."

"Oh." She dropped her stare to the table. "How long will you be in the city? I forgot to ask."

"A few more days."

Her face fell.

"Why?" His heart fluttered. "You hoping it will be more?"

She lifted her chin, shaking her shoulders. "No."

He didn't buy that one bit. She was starting to become attached to him as much as he had her.

The umbrellas above their heads, which shielded customers from the sun, shifted a bit in the muggy breeze.

Grace giggled, wincing.

"What?" Adam drank some of his tangy pineapple juice. "Why are you giggling?"

"It's you." She covered her mouth as she chewed. "You keep staring at me."

"Well, you're a beautiful woman."

"Stop." She laughed under her hand. "I don't want you watching me eat. Look at the mountains."

He turned his head away for a second then faced her again. "Nah, I'm good."

She snickered, wiping her mouth.

"You're amazing, Grace. You deserve the world."

"Many men have promised that to me." She waved her fork, swallowing. "But I don't want a man to give me anything, Adam."

"I doubt that." He sat back. "What about love? Don't you want *that*?"

"Romantic love is an illusion." She drew lines in her food with her fork. "At least for people like me."

"That's ridiculous. You telling me you've never been in love?"

"Where I come from, love is a luxury I can't afford. Other things take precedence. Like survival."

"So? Love has nothing to do with where we come from or what we've gone through. If love is coming, it's coming. We have no power over Cupid's arrow. If we did, we wouldn't let ourselves be so tortured by relationships or allow our hearts to be torn into shreds. People can't control love. It controls *you*. Plus, it always comes when you least expect it."

He caught the glimmer in her eye, which suggested she'd gotten the hint that he might've been talking about *them*.

"You've had a special love?" she asked. "One more important than the others?"

"Ronnie." He wiggled his mouth. "Veronica. My wife."

"Wife?" Grace gaped. "You're married?"

"Separated." He squeezed his cup. "About seven months."

"What happened?"

"She fell out of love with me." He shrugged, eyes watering. "Met a guy at her job who swept her off her feet and paid more attention to her than she felt I did."

"Is that true?"

"Guess so." His voice cracked from emotion. "I put all my time into the GHF, and I didn't realize Ronnie felt like she was just waiting on the sidelines. She thought I'd pull further away from the organization, but I got more into it. It put a huge strain on our marriage, me traveling all the time, but I love doing this and helping people."

Grace smiled.

"I love knowing I did something to make someone's life better."

She patted his hand. "I'm sorry, Adam. It's her loss."

"She loves someone else. It is what it is."

"Do you still love her?"

"I'll always love Ronnie. Once you're married, that person becomes a part of you. But we don't belong together and I accept that. I just want her to be happy. Besides, in all the time I've been with Ronnie, I've never felt like this."

Grace squeezed his hand. "To new beginnings, aye?"

"Exactly." Adam stared into her glowing eyes. "And I'm ready for them."

CHAPTER TEN

Adam followed Grace upstairs to his hotel room, enjoying every swivel of her body.

She turned from the door, blushing when she caught his stare. "I had a wonderful day, Adam. The most fun I've had in a long time."

"Don't you do this with all your clients?"

"Yes." She'd taken her head wrap off and was now playing with it in her hands. "But it never felt like this."

"Like what?" He leaned against the door, moving closer to her.

"I don't know." She dropped her head.

"You know." He lifted her chin. "You feel what I feel. Something you don't understand but you love it all the same."

"I'll come back tonight." She stepped back from the door. "Do you like to dance?"

"I like anything if I do it with you."

"There's a club I like to go to. It's not fancy, but I want to take you there. We'll have fun."

"I'd love that."

She turned to leave, and he put his arm around her waist. "I'm not done with you yet."

She tucked in her lips. "Is that so?"

He unlocked the door and pulled her over the threshold.

"What is this?"

He pushed her against the door. "This is me taking control." He kissed down her dress, pulling it up as he got on his knees.

She moaned, her head wrap slipping from her fingers.

Adam took off her white thong and sniffed the sweet, womanly scent of her bush, widening her legs until his tongue met her clit.

"Mm." Grace threw her leg over his shoulder, rocking as licked her labia. "Oh, Adam." She rubbed her tits, the end of her dress tickling his head. "Ooh."

He didn't lick hard, just tickled her clit with the tip of his tongue.

She gyrated, squeezing his head between her thighs.

He turned his head sideways, getting his tongue further inside her, his dick rising when he saw the pink walls of her vagina.

"Uh-huh." She ran her fingers through his hair. "Please don't stop, Adam."

He sucked until she released, drowning his tongue.

"Oh." Grace went limp, falling over as he held her. "Jesus."

He stood, swooped her into his arms and threw her on the bed face first.

"What are you gonna do?" she mumbled into the bedspread.

"You scared?" He panted, taking off his belt.

"No."

He bounded her wrists with his belt and pulled them over her head. "Don't move." He yanked up her dress, tearing the thin material on one side.

She gasped. "You tore it."

He grinned. "You won't care after this."

Adam kissed around her tight buttocks and spread them, sticking his tongue in her tight asshole.

"Oh, yes." She writhed. "Yes, Adam. My ass. Yes!"

He moaned as he sucked her anus, shocked even that part tasted good. Ass eating disgusted him before he met Ronnie. But after years of her begging him to rim her, he finally had and it had quickly become one of his favorite acts.

He'd thank Ronnie later.

"There!" Grace lifted her head. "Right there, Adam. Oh, I'm coming."

He spit on her ass and spread the moisture from her asshole all the way to her pussy. "God, I want you so bad." He pulled his zipper down so hard he almost tore it. "I'm gonna fuck you in the ass, Grace."

She writhed.

"Is that okay?"

"Yes but get a condom." She wiggled her hips. "Adam."

"I got this." He grabbed his pack of Magnums from his pants.

"Let me see it." She struggled to look over her shoulder and he realized she didn't trust him.

He showed it to her.

"Okay." She sighed, nodding.

"You don't trust me?"

"It's just that some men pretend to wear them and I can't tell."

"Grace." He caressed her side. "I'd never, ever do something so shitty."

She flashed a smile over her shoulder. "I know."

Not wanting the awkward conversation to kill the mood, Adam tore the condom open with his teeth, and slid it on his shaft. "You ready?"

"Yes, yes!" She pushed her face to the bed. "Fuck me, Adam."

He spread her cheeks so wide he could see her little hole pulsating. It had widened since he'd sucked it. To his surprise, it took a minimal amount of tugging and he was inside her. As he pumped, her ass clenched his shaft, squeezing every nerve.

"Yeah." He pulled her arms toward him, yanking the belt as he fucked her. "Ah." Her ass smothered his dick while wetness seeped from her pussy. "You're so wet, Grace. Ah."

"Yes." She bounced her head as he pounded her so hard their skin made slapping noises. "Ooh. Oh!"

Adam pumped, face drowning in sweat. "Grace. Oh!"

****

Grace laughed, laying naked beside Adam on the bed an hour later. "You always asking me so many questions."

He lay on his side on his elbow with his hand propped under his chin. "Tell me about your family and where you come from."

She played with her braids, which she'd swooped to one side. "I come from a village in Kibera, and I have seven brothers and a little sister."

Adam whistled. "Seven brothers? I better treat you right, huh?"

"Life is hard in Kibera, just poverty and grief. You'd be disgusted just seeing pictures of the place, but it is my home and where I learned to survive. Because of that, even with all the problems it has, I love it and I love my family."

He nodded.

"You can't imagine the things I've been through. Nothing was given

easily to me, Adam. I've worked for everything. Let me show you." She got her phone off the nightstand and Googled Kibera. "This is where I am from."

Adam took one look at the place and his heart bled. To Grace, this was home. To Adam, all he saw was sadness, desperation, and hardship.

Filthy shacks barely standing, using each other for balance. The stench of extreme poverty wafting from the images. A world built on trash, hopelessness and neglect. Neglect by a government that allowed its people to suffer in conditions not fit for a dog.

Adam scrolled through pictures and more and more his pity for the people turned into anger that anyone, even the United States could allow people in the world to live like this.

This was why. These pictures. These villages. This place. Is why Adam was a member of the GHF. He might not have the power to do a damn thing but he'd try. That was a promise.

"I'm gonna help you." He sniffed. "I'm gonna make sure the GHF helps in some kind of way because this isn't right, Grace. No one anywhere in the world should ever have to live like this."

She nodded.

"This isn't living." A tear skated down his cheek. "I don't mean to offend you. This is your home—"

"No." She caressed his arm. "It means the world to me that you care. I agree. This isn't a life for any human."

"I don't understand how people see this and don't care. Governments should protect their people. It's disgusting that you had to live like this. I can't..." He handed her the phone, closing his eyes. "I...I'm so sorry."

"I didn't mean to make you upset."

He wiped his eyes. "I hate seeing humans suffering like this. I don't know anyone with a heart that could look at those pictures and not cry. Not feel just the most sadness they've ever felt."

"You are a good man, Adam." She stroked his hair. "I wish there were more like you in the world but many do not care about others. That's what I saw the minute we met, your heart. It's what makes you who you are."

"In the States, we take so much for granted. In many countries, running water is a *luxury* when a basic right of any human should be access to clean water. It humbles you to see how others live."

"Before I moved to the city, I didn't even know what a toilet was." Grace laughed. "We used the resources God gave us and felt that was all we needed."

He kissed her arm. "I admire you for doing what you can to help your family."

She looked ahead. "I'm not proud of what I do, but it's the only choice I've had."

"Don't give up on your dreams, Grace. I know you want more."

"Course I want more. No one *wants* to sell themselves, but it's the hand that's been given to me. When I get to the States, I'm going to work in the medical field."

"A doctor?"

"A medical technician." She straightened her shoulders, pride bursting from her eyes. "My parents instilled in us the importance of education because without that you have nothing. They want me to have way more than they ever could."

Adam laid his head on the pillow. "I didn't go to college."

"You didn't?"

"No, I thought about it, but my mom couldn't afford it and I didn't want a bunch of student loans."

"What do you do?"

"I work for a lawn car service. I'm not raking it in, but it pays the bills. Barely." He chuckled.

"I don't want 'barely', Adam. I want 'success'. You have so much offered to you and you squander it away?"

"I didn't squander anything. Everyone doesn't have to go to college to be successful, Grace."

"Are you successful?" She gestured to him. "Do you want to do lawn service your whole life?"

"Well, no—"

"How about going to school so you can one day own the company you work for, Adam? Look at my circumstances. I refuse to let them stop me, then yours shouldn't stop you." She tapped his chest. "Go to school, Adam. Get student loans, whatever. Better yourself because you only get one chance."

"Wow." He scoffed.

"Did I offend you?"

"No." He pulled her into his arms. "You're amazing, Grace. Simply amazing."

Also by Stacy-Deanne

Possessed
Destined
Stripped Series (Books 1-5)
Stripped Series Books 1-3
Stripped Series (Books 4-6)

Tate Valley Romantic Suspense Series
Now or Never
Now or Never
Chasing Forever
Chasing Forever
Sinner's Paradise
Sinner's Paradise
Last Dance
Last Dance
Tate Valley The Complete Series

The Bruised Series
Bruised
Captivated
Disturbed
Entangled
Twisted

The Good Girls and Bad Boys Series
Who's That Girl?
You Know My Name
Hate the Game

The Studs of Clear Creek County
The White Knight Cowboy
The Forlorn Cowboy

Standalone
The Seventh District
Gonna Make You Mine
Empty
Gonna Make You Mine
Protecting Her Lover
What Grows in the Garden
Love is a Crime
On the Way to Heaven
Open Your Heart
Open Your Heart
A Matter of Time
Hero
Outside Woman
The Watchers
Harm a Fly
Harm a Fly
An Unexpected Love
You're the One
Worth the Risk
Hawaii Christmas Baby
The Best Christmas Ever
Prey
The Good Girls and Bad Boys Series
Bruised Complete Series

Tate Valley Complete Series

The Princess and the Thief

The Little Girl

The Stranger

Oleander

Seducing Her Father's Enemy

Love & Murder: 3-Book Romantic Suspense Starter Set

Paradise

Stalked by the Quarterback

Stripped Complete Series

Tell Me You Love Me

Secrets of the Heart

Five Days

Off the Grid

Sex in Kenya

Fatal Deception

A Cowboy's Debt

Billionaires for Black Girls Set (1-4)

A Savior for Christmas

The Samsville Setup

Trick The Treat

The Cowboy She Left in Wyoming

Theodore's Ring

Wrangle Me, Cowboy

The Billionaire's Slave

The Cowboy's Twin

Everwood County Plantation

Billionaires for Black Girls Set 5-7

The Lonely Hearts of San Sity

Stranded with Billionaire Grumpy Pants

Also by Venus Ray

Lightning Source UK Ltd.
Milton Keynes UK
UKHW030633200922
409139UK00001B/65